SAM

The Tale of a Chesapeake Bay Rockfish

By Kristina Henry
Illustrated by Jeff Dombek

4880 Lower Valley Road · Atglen, PA 19310

With a swish of shimmery scales, Sam swam in circles in the warm, green water. It was early summer, and for Sam that meant swimming in the Chesapeake Bay—his home during the summer months.

Sam was a rockfish. To anyone other than a resident of the Eastern Shore of Maryland, Sam was a striped bass. But locally, he was a rockfish, both to the other inhabitants of the deep and to the people who lived above the water.

Sam was old and very, very big. He had long stripes, dark blue or gray, depending on how you looked at him, along both sides of his silvery body. His eyes were dark. But most beautiful of all was his magnificent tail!

Every spring, Sam and others like him returned to the Bay from warmer waters down south. Sam often chose to swim in a less crowded place than the other rockfish. His favorite place of all was under the dock of a restaurant that sat right on the water.

Sam knew from memory (you see, rockfish have excellent memories) that this restaurant was very popular with the locals. And if he timed it right, they would be eating dinner when he got there. He would swim right up to the side where the people sat and roll on his back. This always got him a few crackers and other leftovers the people did not eat. There was only one small problem.

Sam had some competition. Some of the local ducks and swans liked to eat there too. So . . . Sam had to arrive early every evening to get first dibs on all of the tasty morsels. But Sam also had a secret weapon! As a fish, he could dive down deep. And usually, when people dropped food in the water for the ducks and swans, unless they caught it with their beaks, it fell directly to the bottom.

Swoosh! Off Sam would go, down to the bottom, and *Chomp!* He would eat up all of the delicacies waiting for him.

The days passed like this all summer long, and Sam got fat. He could float by the surface lazily and let the current take him along in its drift. Then, suddenly, he would roll on his stomach and dart down deep, doing an underwater flip! It was fun being a rockfish here in the Chesapeake Bay. Sam could swim all day and eat to his heart's content all night. French fries, bread, crackers. And best of all, the water was warm and salty. Life was perfect indeed!

In fact, life was so perfect for Sam, and he was having such a wonderful time, that he did not pay any attention to his size. He continued to play in the water. He would swim directly under the ducks and swans and nibble on their feet, gently pulling them.

"Now shoo, Sam!" the swans would say, peering down at him, their majestic necks bent ever so slightly.

"Catch me!" he would cry, and then swim off at full speed.

Well, it just so happened on one of these playful occasions that Sam swam off so swiftly and suddenly, he did not look where he was going.

And what do you think happened?

Sam swam directly into a big green bottle that was resting on the sandy bottom.

Klunk! went his head!

"Ouch!" said Sam. He lay there stunned for a moment. Everything around him was green and blurry. Sam thought that he must have really hit his nose hard against the object. Then, when he tried to move, he realized he was stuck. He pushed.

"Aaagh!" he cried. Sam was motionless. He was *really* stuck.

He pushed again. And this time, he twisted his body as much as he could, until finally, he could turn around. Now, he was facing the tip of the bottle where the opening was. He could see the outside world just a little through the tiny hole. But still, the water was so murky that not even the swans, with their elegantly long necks, could see where he was.

"Help!" cried Sam. But that did not work, because by the time his cries reached the surface, they were only bubbles.

"This is no use!" said Sam to himself. And there he remained, stuck inside the old, discarded bottle at the bottom of the Chesapeake Bay.

After a few moments, the tide started to go out, slowly. Sam felt the bottle move on the sandy bottom. His spirits lifted.

"Maybe I will float to the top and the swans will help me get out of this thing," he thought to himself.

But soon he realized that he was simply too heavy with the bottle, and that the only direction in which he was going was out toward the sea. This did not really worry Sam, because the water was his home. What worried him was that he could spend the rest of his life in this green capsule, only allowed to watch everything around him, and no longer participating in this community beneath the surface.

Sam closed his eyes and dreamed of his future inside the bottle. He dreamed of other, smaller fish swimming past him and laughing at him.

"Look at that big old rockfish!" they would cry. "He got himself stuck inside of that thing," they would giggle. And then, with a gentle swish of their collective tails, they would be off, in a dash of bright colors and a flurry of tiny bubbles.

Suddenly, Sam felt something pulling him!

"Oh, leave me alone," he cried. "Please!" He was being pulled faster and faster. The movement woke him up, and Sam realized he had been dreaming.

But he was still moving! He looked around as much as he could. And all he could see was water rushing past him at a frightening speed. There were bubbles everywhere.

As he sat in his green bottle, he thought for sure something horrible awaited him.

"What could be pulling me so fast?" he asked himself.

With that question barely out of his mouth, Sam began to see the surface of the water. It got brighter and brighter. And before he could think another thought, he was pulled into the air, and was flying above the water.

Sam's eyes widened. His mouth formed the letter O! And just as he looked ahead to try to see what was happening, Sam saw a big green hand grab the bottle with him in it!

"Well, well, what do we have here?" said a strange voice.

Sam stared at a man in a boat who was holding him with his huge green hand.

"Looks like I've caught myself a prize!" said the man, smiling.

Sam was shaking. Not only was this the worst day of his life, it looked like it might be the last! Sam had

He continued to stare at the fisherman with the big green hands.

"Well, you certainly are the biggest rock I've *ever* seen! And how did you get yourself caught in this thing?" asked the man in disbelief.

Sam's shaking increased. His eyes were open wide with terror.

"Well, you look like you've been around here too long to be caught. I'm gonna let you go today," said the man to Sam.

"My friends won't believe this when I tell them, so we'll just have to keep this our little secret, hhmmm? I'm sure you wouldn't want your friends to know about this either." And, as he said these things, the man began to wrap something around the bottle. All at once it was dark for Sam, but somehow he knew that the man was helping him.

Sam felt something hitting the side of the bottle. But it didn't hurt, and before he knew it, he was free! The man was holding him in his big gloved hands, which were no longer green.

The man held Sam up in front of him.

"Wow!" he exclaimed. "You sure are a whopper!" And he whistled a long, slow whistle.

"Now go on before I change my mind."

And with that said, the fisherman gently placed
Sam back into the water and held onto him until he
was sure that Sam was all right. Then he let go.

Sam raced to the bottom, looking straight ahead.
He could not believe what had just happened.

When he reached the lower depths, Sam slowed
down a bit. He knew where he was going, but he
wanted to enjoy the swim. It felt good to move his fins
and wiggle his huge tail. He turned his head slightly
and looked back at his tail. Then, remembering what
had gotten him into trouble in the first place, he
decided to watch where he was going—and headed
toward his favorite spot.

When he got there, he swam toward the surface.

"Where were you?" asked the swans.

"I got stuck in a big, green bottle, and a fisherman caught me and let me go!" he said.

"Sure!" said the ducks, quacking.

All at once, Sam dove down toward the bottom just in time to snatch a cracker.

"Mmmmm! Mmmmm!" he said to himself.

And the evening had just begun.